BERRY BLAST

POWDER PELLETS

Sheila

and the Sugar Monster

by Mary Meyer

Illustrated by
AndoTwin

Lights Up Publishing

Pittsburgh, PA • USA

Lights Up Publishing
PO Box 14505
Castle Shannon Blvd.
Pittsburgh, PA 15234
lightsuppublishing.com
lightsuppublishing@gmail.com

Printed and bound in the United States of America

First Edition

10 9 8 7 6 5 4 3 2 1

LCCN 2016947871

ISBN 978-0-692-75557-0

This book was expertly produced by Book Bridge Press
www.bookbridgepress.com

book bridge press

For David, Will, Ben, and the Wupses—with love and thankfulness

Special thanks to Mom for reading me all those books,
and to Dad for encouraging me to write
—M. M.

by Ben Meyer, age 9

If I had to pick my very favorite food of all time it would definitely be **Coco Cookie Crunch** cereal with chocolate milk. Or maybe cupcakes with vanilla frosting and sprinkles. Or chocolate chip cookies. Or *Fruit Punch Powder Pellets.* Or **Berry Blast** bubble gum. Or butter pecan ice cream. Or strawberry shortcake. Or licorice or fudgcicles or popsicles or caramels or gummy fish or marshmallows or toffee chews or lollipops or cherry sours or *ahhhhhh!* I just can't decide!

Treats make me soooo happy!
And so *fast!* I can run like a cheetah!
Watch how fast I can spin! *Fyoom! Fyoom! Fyoom!*

I can even
flyyyyyy...

What happened? What time is it?
I know! Time for more candy!
"Mom, can I have some c-a-n-d-y?"
"No. You can have an a-p-p-l-e."
"What? No! I want candy! Just one
little, tiny piece of candy.
Pleeeeeease?"
"You can have one little, tiny piece
of broccoli."
"NoooOOOO!"

"I see the sugar monster is visiting again."

"No, it isn't!"

"Well, I thought it was because you're getting awfully gr—"

"No, I'm not!"

"Grum—"

"No, I'm NOT!"

"Grump—"

"I'M." "NOT." "GRUMPY!"

I wonder why Mom is being strange today. I bet Mrs. Merriweather told her I was acting up at school again. Well, you would act up too if you had to sit as still as a statue all day. And listen to the most **boring** stuff in the world. And do the most **boring** work in the universe. And sit by the most **annoying** human ever to exist, Penelope Pumice, who tells you to shush every five seconds.

At least I still got to have my hot cocoa with mini marshmallows before bed.

The next day I tried my hardest to pay attention to Mrs. Merriweather and to ignore Penelope, but she wouldn't stop shushing me!

So I **shush**ed **her**.

And then the principal shushed me and sent me home from school early.

And that did not shush Mom.

If that wasn't bad enough, Mom and Dad took me to
see the doctor!

They told her about the so-called sugar monster
and the *Penelope Pumice* incident.

And that's when things got really rotten. When we got home, Mom took out a garbage bag and started to throw away **all my favorite foods.**

Sayonara, sugar.

Mom rolled the garbage can to the end of the driveway.
"Bring it back **right now!** Or I'm going to **run away!**"
"Where will you go?"
"I don't know. Maybe Florida."
"How will you get there?"
"I'll take the bus."

"How will you pay for it?"
"Can I borrow some money?"
"No."
"Why?"
"Because I love you, and I would miss you terribly if you left."
"Then you better make me a *cupcake*."
"Sorry, no cupcake, Cupcake."

I ran to my room. I threw my books off the shelf. I threw my toys against the wall. I **punched** my pillow until I was too tired to punch anymore. Then I cried until I fell asleep.

At dawn, I watched the garbage collector dump all my treats into the truck. My Coco Cookie Crunch was being mixed with mushy, moldy apple cores and stinky doggy doo-doo bags. Gone, gone, gone.

I pulled the covers over my head and cried myself back to sleep.

I dreamed about delicious food. A castle made of ice cream and **cakes and candy** and cookies and milkshakes. I was just about to bite into a warm chocolate chip cookie

crown when Mom invaded my dream. "Too much sugar! Have some broccoli instead."
Ahhhhhhh!
What a nightmare.

At least I still had my secret candy stash. **Nooooooo!** No more treats. No more sugar. No more fun. Life had lost its flavor.

When Mom made me come downstairs for breakfast, my Coco Cookie Crunch bowl was filled with a glop of oatmeal. **Blech. Barf. Boring.** There was no way I was eating that.

And when I unpacked my lunch at school, it was just as bad.

Dinner didn't get any better.

"Are you trying to kill me?"

"I'm trying to help you."

"But I'm **starving!**"

"Then eat."

"I can't eat that. I'll throw up!"

"That's the sugar monster talking."

"But I haven't had **any sugar!**"

"That's why it's upset."

"Ahhhhhhh!"

"When the sugar monster is gone, you'll understand."

"THERE! IS! NO! SUGAR! MONSTER!"

The next morning, there was a plate of brown toast, scrambled eggs with green stuff in them, and fruit waiting for me. **Boring. Blech. Barf.** This sugar shakedown was getting out of hand.

But I was really, **really** hungry. I ate the fruit. And the toast. And the eggs. But I didn't like it. Not one bit. After that, things started to get extremely weird.

That night a loud noise woke me up. It sounded like a dinosaur clomping past my room. I heard it *thump* down the stairs. Then the front door swung open and snapped shut. I looked out my window to see who had left.

"No way!"

The sugar monster!

It slumped down my driveway. When it got to the end, it turned around and waved good-bye.

Then things got even weirder.

Some of Mom's food actually started to taste **pretty good.** School became kind of interesting. And the most surprising thing of all, Penelope Pumice decided to stop being so annoying.

Life with the sugar monster sure was tasty.

But life without it is even sweeter.

I think I should warn Penelope, though. I'm pretty sure
I saw the sugar monster moving into her house last night.

Mary Meyer lives in Pittsburgh, Pennsylvania, with her husband, David, and their two sons, Will and Ben. She loves them even more than lollipops. A sugar monster used to live with them too, but it moved out a few years ago. Now there's more space for her two puppies (who enjoy eating shoes much more than sugar). This is Mary's first picture book. Visit her anytime at marymeyerbooks.com.

Nicola Anderson (a.k.a. AndoTwin) crafts imaginary worlds from her home studio in Manchester, UK, while her two dogs fight for her lap. She has been illustrating since she could hold a crayon in her hand; professionally, since 2001. She has created many picture books, apps, games, and comics for numerous publishers.